Published in Great Britain and the United States 1986 by
Magnolia Books, an imprint of
Webb & Bower (Publishers) Limited
9 Colleton Crescent, Exeter, Devon EX2 4BY

First published in dossier form 1937 by Hutchinson & Co (Publishers) Limited
Republished in facsimile form 1980 by Webb & Bower (Publishers) Limited
This edition Copyright © Webb & Bower (Publishers) Limited 1986

Printed and bound in Hong Kong by Mandarin Offset Marketing (HK) Limited

To

The Assistant Commissioner,

    i/c Anti-Terrorist Operations.

Sir,

    I have to report that at 11.45 p.m. last night Detective-Sergeant P. M. Flanagan, who has been loaned to us by the Free State Police, recognized the terrorist Sean Connolly entering the Milky Way Club, Curzon Street, Mayfair.

    It was not previously known to us that Connolly was in this country, and, in fact, it was believed that he had retired altogether from active participation in the I.R.A. organization, as, having become a sufferer from chronic asthma, he left Ireland in November 1937 to settle in South Africa.

    However, his past record as a leader of the most fanatical and dangerous type makes it highly probable that he has become active again now that he has returned to Great Britain.

    As he is either travelling on a forged passport or, if on his own, lacks a British visa, we could, of course, deport him at once; but in the hope that he may lead us to certain of his associates, I am having both him and the Club kept under observation.

The Milky Way Club is now run as a de luxe Bottle Party by a very able Russian restaurateur named Serge Orloff. I have applied to the Foreign Department for his dossier.

I have the honour to be, Sir,

Your obedient servant,

J. D. MacKechnie

Detective Inspector, Special Branch.

New Scotland Yard,

Room 208b.

13.5.39.

To

The Assistant Commissioner,

    i/c Anti-Terrorist Operations.

Sir,

Further to my report of the 10th inst., I have now ascertained that the ex-terrorist Sean Connolly is living in furnished apartments kept by a **Mr.** and Mrs. Patrick Murphy at 86, Hertford Street, Park Lane, W.1.

The **Murphys** are Irish born, but of British nationality, **and** have been resident in London since 1932. Mrs. (Kathleen) Murphy runs the house, which has a good connection of monied patrons, who stay there when visiting London, while her husband is a director of, and agent for, a firm of book-match importers. His territory is the Irish Free State, so he **makes** frequent journeys to and from the I.F.S. on business.

Connolly paid a further visit to the Milky Way on Thursday night, and was accompanied by the Murphys. They remained there only three-quarters of an hour, and left, as they had arrived, together.

On Friday, Angela Sullivan was seen there in company with Captain Terrance Boyd-O'Dare, late of **the** Royal Ulster Rifles. He

is on our list of suspects, and she, as you will recall, is the English-born wife of Bryan Sullivan, who recently received a seven-year sentence for his complicity in the Liverpool bomb outrages.

The above facts having given me good reason to suppose that the Milky Way is being used as a permanent centre by a group of the I.R.A., I tackled the proprietor, Serge Orloff, this morning.

Not wishing to arouse the suspicions of the other members of the Club staff, who may be implicated, I did not visit the Club or have Orloff brought in for questioning, but, in company with Detective-Sergeant Spigott, picked him up after the Club closed and he had gone down to do his marketing in Covent Garden.

The three of us adjourned to the lounge of the Strand Palace Hotel, which at that hour is practically deserted, and, over coffee, I told Orloff that we knew of his association with the I.R.A., and intended to have him run out of the country.

Naturally, he denied all knowledge of the Irish terrorists; and said that if any of them were using his Club they came to it by the invitation of other guests, were quite indistinguishable from them, and that he was certainly no party to their activities.

Orloff is the son of a Russian restaurant proprietor of good standing. He was a student at Kharkov University when the Revolution broke out, threw in his lot with the Bolsheviks, and became an ardent disciple of Trotsky's, with whom he worked in close collaboration. On Trotsky's fall in 1928 Orloff fled the country

to save himself from execution by the Stalin-ites. He took
refuge here as a political refugee, and, having maintained a
clean bill ever since, has been allowed to remain.

When I pointed out that we were aware of his old terrorist
activities, and therefore had good reason to assume that he was
still in sympathy with all terrorist movements, he was consider-
ably shaken; but continued to protest his innocence.

At the Milky Way changing is optional, although it is one
of the smartest night-haunts in London, and for the entertainment
of male guests, mainly foreigners who are sent there by the big
hotels, Orloff employs a number of dance hostesses. Theoretically
these women are not supposed to leave the premises until four
o'clock in the morning, but if any of them has a man in tow
Orloff allows them to leave any time after two on payment to him
of a fine of £5.

I informed him that we were aware of this and that, unless
he came clean, I proposed to run him in right away on a charge of
procuring. As a result his place would be closed down, and his
permit to remain in this country would be cancelled. He would
then be deported to Russia where, as a known Trotskyist, he would
be promptly imprisoned on his arrival, and, probably, shot.

On this he went to pieces entirely, implored me not to take
any action against him, and offered to place himself unreservedly
at our disposal if only I would guarantee that he should not be
sent back to the U.S.S.R.

I said that I could guarantee nothing; but that if he could
furnish us with information and assistance which would lead to the
arrest of any members of the I.R.A. now operating in the U.K., the
authorities would be grateful to him, and doubtless show their
gratitude, if occasion arose, in a suitable manner.

He then placed himself unreservedly in my hands, and gave
me the following particulars.

Early in January a German journalist named Heinrich Häuser
came to the Club as a casual visitor. Orloff recognized him
at once as a Trotskyist sympathizer with whom he had worked in
Russia.

Recognition was mutual and Häuser confided that he still
believed the British Empire to be the principal enemy of World
Freedom and was continuing his activities against it through the
I.R.A.. At a further meeting, a few days later, he suggested that
Orloff should also resume work for the cause through this channel

Orloff declares that he no longer believes in the practical
possibility of a World Revolution and, therefore, demurred but,
by an offer of lavish payment, he was finally induced to place
his premises at the disposal of Häuser and his friends.

When they first adopted the Milky Way as a rendezvous
Häuser's group consisted of: his cousin, Karl Finigan (Irish,
German mother), Madame Pauline Vidor (Polish), Captain Terrance
Boyd-O'Dare (British, native of Ulster), Denis Burke (Irish), Mr.
and Mrs. Patrick Murphy (British, Irish born), Angela Sullivan

(Irish by marriage, British born), William Benson (British) and Henry Wilson (British).

Their number has since been added to from outside by Mademoiselle Ninon de Lys (French), A. B. Masters (British) and Sean Connolly (Irish).

Also by Serge Orloff himself (Russian), his band leader and part-owner of the Milky Way, Tony Pendennys (British), and Carlotta Casado (Spanish) who arranges the Cabarets at the Club.

The cell, therefore, now consists of 16 members - 11 men and 5 women.

Orloff states that they all visit the Club singly or in couples at least once a week, for the purpose of passing information one to another, and that at intervals of about three weeks a general meeting is held at which all 16 members are present.

The only addresses of members he could give me were: Tony Pendennys, 54, Gilbert Street, Grosvenor Square, W.1, and Carlotta Casado, 10b, Willingham Mansions, Maida Vale, W.9.

I informed him that, if he wished to secure our complete goodwill, he must obtain the addresses of the other members of the group for us, but this, he declared, it was quite impossible for him to do.

In a great state of agitation he assured me that, if any of the Irish terrorists suspected that he was spying on them, they would kill him without hesitation.

My considered opinion is that Orloff is an unwilling par-
ticipant in the I.R.A. organization and that his one desire is
to be left in peaceful possession of his Club.

The Milky Way is well attended, has excellent Cabarets, a
good reputation and is largely frequented by society people; so
there is reason to suppose that it is a paying proposition. I
do not believe that Orloff would have risked its closure, the
possibility of a heavy prison sentence and, if repatriated to
Russia, his life, solely for the ideals which animated his
youth - or even for a certain amount of money. The probability
is that his old associate, Heinrich Häuser, had something on
him from the past, and forced him to co-operate.

If I am right, the chances are that Orloff is not regarded
as completely trustworthy; in which case any special display of
interest by him in any other member of the group would be fatal,
as, once their suspicions were aroused, they would disperse in
any case, even if they did not kill him.

Realizing Orloff's difficulties, I suggested that he should
plant Detective-Sergeant Spigott in the Club and point out
members of the I.R.A. group to him as occasion arose, as this
would enable us to identify and trace them without Orloff having
to act in any way that might arouse their suspicions.

With considerable reluctance Orloff agreed to this on the
understanding that, in the event of a prosecution against the
group, he should be regarded as having turned King's Evidence

and that, subject to his continued good conduct, no steps should be taken to deport him.

Orloff has promised to frame a quarrel with his doorman on Monday and, after the man's dismissal, Detective-Sergeant Spigott is to be engaged in his place.

Spigott will pass us full descriptions of all group members indicated to him by Orloff as these, in turn, next visit the Club.

I shall then have them traced to their present addresses and kept under permanent observation. It is to be hoped that we shall then be able to net the whole group directly we can formulate a serious charge against any member of it

I have the honour to be, Sir,

Your obedient servant,

J. D. MacKechnie

Detective Inspector, Special Branch.

To

The Assistant Commissioner,

  i/c Anti-Terrorist Operations.

Sir,

    Further to my report of the 13th inst., Detective-Sergeant Spigott was duly installed as doorman at the Milky Way Club on Monday, the 15th.

    On information received from him we have now succeeded in tracing all members of the I.R.A. group which is using the premises and they are now all under surveillance.

    Among them is Rory O'Leary, now passing under the name of Denis Burke, an extremely dangerous fanatic who, you will recall, is wanted by us in connection with the attempt to destroy Hammersmith Bridge.　As cover he has obtained a job with C. V. Kennett and Sons, a firm of picture-frame makers in Great Marlborough Street, and he is now living in rooms at 108, Acacia Road, St. John's Wood, N.W.8.　For the time being, of course, it is expedient to leave him on a string, but it is highly satisfactory to know that we have run him to earth at last.

    The Murphys, Connolly, Boyd-O'Dare, Finigan and the woman Sullivan are all fanatics on the Irish question but, outwardly, law-abiding citizens;　and we have no charge which we could bring against any of them at the moment except possibly, in some cases, for passport irregularities.

Madame Vidor is living with Finigan in a furnished flat at Queen Charlotte's Mansions, S.W.1, and is doubtless acting under his influence.

Finigan's German cousin, Heinrich Häuser, is attached to the London branch of Dragenberg's World Press Agency and his permit is in order.

Too much weight must not be placed on the fact that he was a Communist when he worked with Orloff in Russia and still appears to be pro-Communist. Many Germans have seen good reason to change their politics in the last twelve years and I do not believe that Dragenberg's would be allowed to employ any German with anti-Nazi sympathies.

As you are aware, we have good reason to believe that the I.R.A. are being largely subsidized by secret grants from foreign Governments whose objective is to create trouble here. Häuser's apparent Communist leanings would give him some cover from the attentions of our anti-espionage people, but I consider it highly probable that he is actually a foreign agent and supplies the funds of the I.R.A. that meet at the Milky Way; having contacted them through his cousin, Karl Finigan.

Ninon de Lys is a recent recruit to the group. She is a professional dancer of some standing and, until a short time ago, was appearing at the London Casino. Boyd-O'Dare is a man of unusually strong personality and appears to have taken her fancy to such an extent that she now seems to be completely

under his influence.   She has a considerable number of important
male acquaintances and, in my opinion, Boyd-O'Dare is using her
as a stool pigeon to secure certain information that he requires.

Henry Wilson turns out to be our old acquaintance ''Scab''
Wilson, the safe-blower, who has done several spells inside and
was last released from Dartmoor Prison on November 4th, 1938.
When Scab is outside, his less spectacular activities consist
of stealing sticks of dynamite from legitimate stores and
indulging in the dangerous practice of converting them into
''soup''.

The I.R.A. have apparently taken him on owing to his expert
knowledge of explosives and it may reasonably be assumed that
his interest is a purely commercial one.   It doubtless pays him
better to make bombs for the I.R.A. and limit his risk to their
manufacture, than go the whole hog and indulge in further safe-
blowings.   But, for some reason as yet unknown, he appears to
have a deadly grudge against Orloff.   Spigott reports that on
the one occasion he saw them meet they were like cat and dog
together.

A. B. (or ''Mug'') Masters is another old lag.   He is a
cat burglar of some proficiency and has, in the past, worked in
conjunction with Scab.   His tie-up with the group is also,
almost certainly, upon a purely financial basis.   He again is
a recent recruit and doubtless Scab was responsible for roping
him in because the group needed someone of his peculiar abilities.

William (Big Bill) Benson is an international adventurer.
He fought in the Great War, took to bootlegging from the West
Indies afterwards, fought again in the Paraguay-Bolivian War,
and in the Far East.   Between wars he has been concerned in
gun-running to various countries and, for some time, he ran a
shell-filling plant in China.   His participation in the activities
of the group is doubtless to be accounted for by his lifelong
craving for excitement and a desire to make quick money.
When he last returned to England, he was virtually broke;   and
the I.R.A. people would find his knowledge of explosives, gained
in China, invaluable.

It is probable that Scab Wilson and Mug Masters are
employed to steal dynamite, gun-cotton, etc., from engineers'
stores and that Benson assists them in converting the raw
explosives into infernal machines for the use of the terrorists.

This accounts for the motives which have actuated all
members who have joined the group except Tony Pendennys and
Carlotta Casado;   but to them I will refer later.

Orloff has informed Spigott that a full meeting of the
group has been called for the night of Tuesday, the 23rd, to
plan a further series of outrages.   He has also made an important
disclosure about the Club premises.

The Milky Way backs on to No. 94, Shepherd's Market;
which is an empty shop.   The flats above have a separate
entrance, No. 94a.   (Sketch plan enclosed herewith.)

SHEPHERDS MARKET.

| 91. | 91 A | 92. | 92 A | 93. | 93 A | 94. EMPTY SHOP | 94 A | 95. | 95 A | 96. | 96 A |

SECRET ROOM

KITCHENS

STAFF W.C's

CELLAR

PASSAGE

STORE ROOM

AREA

AREA

MILKY WAY

CLOAK ROOMS

HALL

OFFICE

FLORIST

HAT SHOP

CURZON STREET

NOTE.
ORLOFF'S PREMISES ARE THICKLY OUTLINED.

No. 94, which consists of the shop, a room in its rear adjacent to the Club storeroom, and basement, is held on a seven year lease by Orloff; and at the end of a passage to the left of the Club storeroom there is a masked door by means of which access can be had through the partition wall of the Club to the room in the rear of the shop.

Orloff states that all group meetings are held in this secret room, which he cleans up himself each time after it has been used, and that it is there the terrorists manufacture and store their bombs.

The shop in Shepherd's Market is boarded up and its entrance is locked and barred; so the only means of reaching the secret room, which has no windows, is through the Club by way of the masked door. Orloff alone has a key to this and passes each member of the group through it as they arrive, locking it again after them and entering himself with the last comer.

Questioned by Spigott as to his reason for relocking the door each time he has passed one of his friends through it into the room, his answers were vague and unsatisfactory; but I believe this gives us the key to the reason for Orloff's having become involved with the I.R.A.

He has had the shop premises in Shepherd's Market for close on three years and, I suggest, was using the back room as a dope store. If I am right in my assumption, the following probabilities emerge:

(1)   When Heinrich Häuser arrived on the scene in January Orloff probably confided to this old associate of his that he was running dope, and took him to the secret room.

Häuser saw at once that the Milky Way and its concealed annex would make an excellent centre for the I.R.A. group of which he was a member and, by a threat of laying information with us that Orloff was a dope-trafficker, forced him to place his premises at the group's disposal.

(2)   Orloff agreed under pressure but refused to surrender the key of the store or have duplicates made; fearing that, if he did, certain habitual criminals among the group, such as Scab Wilson, might pillage his stock of illicit drugs.

This would account for his caution in conducting each member of the group to the masked door, letting them through and locking the door after them.   They cannot get out through the locked shop entrance in Shepherd's Market or back to the Club, until he lets them out after each meeting.   In this way he is able to keep an eye on his stock and assure himself that nothing has been stolen, before they leave the room.

(3)   This brings me to the probable reason why Tony Pendennys and Carlotta Casado have been drawn into the I.R.A. group.

They are Orloff's principal assistants in running the Milky Way and he has assured Spigott that they are the only two members of his staff who know of the existence of the secret room.

Pendennys, I now learn from Records, was tried but acquitted on a dope-smuggling charge in Marseilles in 1936 and the Casado woman is the sister of ''Spanish Joe'' who was deported last month for being concerned in a similar affair; both of which facts tie up with my theory that Orloff was using the room for the purpose of trafficking in illicit drugs.

I suggest that when Häuser learned that the two knew of the secret room he realised that they would prove a danger to the activities of his I.R.A. group and, to counter this, forced them to join it by using similar threats to those which I postulate he employed with Orloff.

Pendennys earns good money as a band leader so it is un-likely that he would willingly risk a heavy prison sentence for a nominal financial gain and, normally, he is not the type who would be the least interested in political movements of any kind; so, obviously, some form of pressure must have been exerted to rope him in.

Carlotta Casado, on the other hand, is a Spanish refugee, an artistic visionary and intellectual, and was, at one time, a prominent Barcelona anarchist and member of the F.A.I. She therefore probably met the overtures of the Irish terrorists with immediate sympathy.

(4) A further fact that points to the secret room having been used as a dope store is that Orloff made no mention of the room until he told Spigott of it yesterday.

Orloff saw the absolute necessity for giving us the fullest possible co-operation, if he wished to escape deportation, at my interview with him on the 13th. He must have realised then that as soon as we had collected sufficient data about the I.R.A. group we should raid the Club and his secret room would almost certainly be discovered.

To keep in with us, therefore, it was of the first importance that he should disclose the existence of the room to us himself. He has now done so, but he held up the information for a week in order, I suggest, that during that time he might remove any dope he had stored there; since, had it been discovered in a raid, we should have been compelled to prosecute and deport him.

Now that we have identified all members of the group I propose to carry out a raid on the Milky Way when they have all assembled in the room behind the Club for their meeting on Tuesday night.

I have instructed Spigott to install a concealed camera in the reception hall of the Club that night and to take photographs of all members of the group as they enter the premises. In the event of any of them eluding the raiding party we shall then have up-to-the-minute portraits of them all for immediate circulation with their descriptions.

It is to be hoped, however, that we shall net the whole group as it is now quite clear that these people are by no means

an ordinary cell but, almost all having money and position, are, most probably, the central organisation of the whole I.R.A. movement in Britain.

If we are fortunate, the presence of Rory O'Leary, alias Denis Burke, in their midst, together with their being assembled in a room used for the illegal storage of explosives and the manufacture of bombs, should enable us to get them all sentences ranging from three to ten years and thus root out, once and for all, the brains of this subversive movement which is causing us so much trouble.

I have the honour to be, Sir,

Your obedient servant,

J. D. MacKechnie

Detective Inspector, Special Branch.

To

The Assistant Commissioner,

   i/c Anti-Terrorist Operations.

Sir,

     I regret to report that last night's raid on the Milky Way Club was a failure.

     When you are informed of the circumstances I trust you will agree that this was in no way the fault of myself or my subordinates.   An event which could not possibly have been foreseen occurred fifteen minutes before the raid was timed to take place, which resulted in the Club prematurely emptying of its occupants. I refer to the murder of Serge Orloff.

     Orloff had informed Detective-Sergeant Spigott earlier in the day that the I.R.A. group would be fully assembled in the secret room for their meeting by 1 o'clock a.m. and that the meeting would last at least an hour.

     Accordingly, I made arrangements to raid the Club premises from the front at 1.10 a.m. while a strong force of police was to cover No. 94, Shepherd's Market, in case any of the group endeavoured to escape by way of the shop at the back.

     To avoid arousing suspicion, no concentration of police was ordered to take place in the area until 1.8 a.m., when sections of

Curzon Street and Shepherd's Market were to be closed and the vans
containing the raiding party were to drive up to the Club.

At 12.56 a.m. Detective-Officers Goddard and Brent, who
were on observation duty in Curzon Street, report that a com-
motion started in the doorway of the Milky Way and people began
to stream out from the Club on to the pavement.

The two detectives hurried up to investigate but were
forced back by the crowd which was further panicked, at
approximately 12.58 a.m., by a loud explosion, to which I will
refer later.

Waiters and kitchen-hands now mingled with the Club guests
who were fighting to get out of its entrance.   Goddard was
knocked down and trampled on and, by the time Brent had got him
on his feet again, the entire mob had rapidly dispersed, mainly
towards Piccadilly.

Goddard and Brent then entered the Club, where they found
Detective-Sergeant Spigott lying unconscious in the hallway.
Otherwise the Club was empty, except for the body of Orloff which
was lying in the passage leading to the masked door.   He had been
shot twice through the back, and was dead when they found him.

A few moments later I arrived with my raiding party, was
informed of what had occurred, and also that an explosion had
taken place in Shepherd's Market, wrecking the shop front of
No. 94.

The masked door between the Club and the secret room was

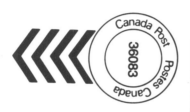
...ck of Orloff's hand; being

... chain which went round his

...dy herewith and it would

...as he was about to admit

...ary type upon which keys

...ly welded so that the key

...ain was secured round

...only 17 inches and so was

...the key in the lock, which

is 64 inches ... ...rloff fell shot. To

lift up his heavy body and get the key in the lock that way

would have been too difficult and cumbersome a task for the

murderer to perform in the very limited time at his disposal

once the people in the Club and adjacent kitchen had been

alarmed by the shooting.

It is certain, therefore, that the murderer did not pass

through the door into the secret room and escape via Shepherd's

Market but must have bolted back and, mingling with the alarmed

crowd in the Club, left with them by the Curzon Street entrance.

Not wishing to move the body until the Police Surgeon had

made his primary examination and the usual photographs been taken,

I went round to Shepherd's Market, at once, as the only means

of reaching the secret room open to me.

The door of No. 94 was still standing and secured. I found that it had actually been nailed up on the inside as well as locked and bolted. But the boarded-up window of the shop had been blown clean out, and ingress or exit over the exposed window display shelf presented no difficulty whatever.

I found the shop unfurnished, also the basement which I visited later; but the back room was fully furnished. It had obviously been recently occupied and its occupants had bolted from it in such a hurry that they had left a number of their possessions behind.

A full list of the room's contents will be forwarded later, but it includes a number of sticks of dynamite of the type used for quarry blasting, a number of hand-made detonators, fourteen complete bombs of amateur construction, empty tins and cheap fibre suitcases for containing same, a packing-case three-quarters full of alarm clocks, two automatic pistols calibre 3 m.m., 108 rounds of ammunition, a collection of maps, mainly of London, and tracings of various plans, one of which I identified as that of Lotts Road Power Station.

It is of the first importance to establish as far as possible which members of the group were in the secret room at the time the murder was committed; and, with this in mind, I am enclosing a photograph of the table round which the occupants of the room were presumably sitting.

Regarding the items shown: The woman's bag is of grey crêpe de Chine. It contained a handkerchief without initial, £2.7.4 in notes and cash, a compact filled with Magnolia shade powder, a bill from Selfridge's for stockings ''3 prs. £1.0.9'', a Guerlain lipstick, five cuttings from the ''Liverpool Post'' and ''Liverpool Echo'' regarding the recent bomb outrages there, a twenty packet of Player's with eleven cigarettes remaining in it and a partially used book of matches bearing an advertisement for the Hungaria Restaurant.

The top hat is a brand new one, supplied by Scotts of Bond Street, size 7½.

The cigarette case is engine-turned silver with a raised R.U.R. crest in gold and enamel and contains 4 Goldflake and 3 Balkan Bairam cigarettes.

The remaining contents of eight glasses are: of five Whisky and Soda, of one Gin and Soda, of one neat Jamaica Rum, and of one plain Soda.

Of the Exhibits, which I despatch herewith:

A, B, C and D were recovered from the table.

E, F, G and H were recovered from the waste-paper basket.

I was dusted from a leather chair seat.

J was found caught in a small split in the woodwork of one of the chair backs.

K, L, M and N were recovered from the floor.

Everything is so smothered in finger-prints, old and new,

that we cannot hope for anything from this source until the experts have had several days to analyse them, but their conclusions may prove useful as corroborative evidence later.

On my return to the Milky Way by its proper entrance in Curzon Street, Police Surgeon Dr. A. C. Entwhistle reported to me that his preliminary examination of the body had shown that Orloff must have died almost instantly from a bullet that entered his heart.

A shell from one of the two bullets with which he was shot (Exhibit O herewith) was found in the passage and establishes the fact that the murderer had used a .22 in. automatic.

The small calibre, suitable for carrying in a handbag, suggests the possibility that the murderer may have been a woman.

Doctor Entwhistle handed to me a small screw of paper (Exhibit P herewith), found in the dead man's right-hand trouser pocket.

This carries a warning message, which obviously comes from one of the group and makes it quite clear that we may rule out any suggestion that one of Orloff's staff or a casual guest at the Club killed him on account of some private quarrel.

Detective-Sergeant Spigott recovered consciousness at 1.3 a.m. but on my first arrival at the Club was still severely shaken, so I sent him back to the Yard to write out his statement, and insert it here in order to preserve continuity in this report.

C O P Y

To : Detective Inspector

J. D. MacKechnie,

Special Branch.

Sir,

Having been detailed for special duty since the 15th inst.
as door-porter at the Milky Way Club, Curzon Street, I arrived
there in accordance with routine at 9.30 p.m. last night.

The Club was then empty except for waiters preparing tables
and kitchen staff at their work, inside.   I therefore had ample
opportunity while unobserved to secrete a camera, as I had been
instructed to do, among the gear at the back of my desk.

Orloff arrived at 9.55.   He appeared well and cheerful but
only exchanged a few words with me as it had been agreed that,
to avoid arousing suspicion, we should never talk except as boss
and man while on the Club premises.

I did not take a photograph of him as I knew that we had
a number, including several recent snaps, already in the
possession of Records.

A few moments later the band came in: the last of them
to do so being their leader, Tony Pendennys.   He is always a
nervy customer but last night he appeared particularly agitated
and asked me at once if Orloff was there yet.   Upon my saying

that he was, Pendennys gave me his usual charming smile and
hurried inside; but not before I had been able to get a picture
of him. (Photograph No. 1).

The dance hostesses, six in number, then turned up, and
Carlotta Casado immediately after them.   She would have passed
me without speaking if I had not said :

''Evening, Miss.   Know anything good for the Gold Cup?''

Racing is not her line so she only shook her head;   but
she paused long enough for me to get the picture of her I wanted.
(Photograph No. 2).

At 10.10 the first guests appeared.   Excluding Orloff,
Pendennys and Carlotta, but including the other 13 members of the
I.R.A. outfit, 82 visitors entered the Club and signed the book
between 10.10 and 12.54.

Most of them were in couples but there was one large party
of 9, and three lots of 4.

About two-thirds of the guests were regular patrons of
the Club whom I had seen at least once before during my tour of
duty there.   Only five of the strangers to me were foreigners;
a French couple who had the appearance of honeymooners, and three
Swedish gentlemen.   The latter enquired if dance hostesses were
available and, on being informed that they were, passed inside.
Both these parties produced the hotel introductions usual in the
case of foreigners and had all the appearance of being on the
spree.

None of the other guests presented any special peculiarities
and I feel confident that Orloff would have tipped me off if any
of them, apart from the I.R.A. people, were anything but normal
night-lifers.

At 11.14 Heinrich Häuser and Angela Sullivan arrived.
To cover the click of the camera I cracked a joke with them just
after they had signed the book and it made them smile.
(Photograph No. 3).

At 11.21 Karl Finigan and Madame Pauline Vidor arrived.
He seemed to be very angry with her but they were talking
together in a language I could not identify.   It was not German
but possibly they were speaking in Polish as that is her nationality.   I cracked the same joke which caused them to break off
their quarrel and they both laughed.   (Photograph No. 4).

At 11.26 Terrance Boyd-O'Dare and Ninon de Lys arrived.
They were very gay, came arm-in-arm and were laughing together.
Without a doubt she has fallen for him and he could twist her
round his little finger.   On passing into the Club she remarked:
''I don't know when I've enjoyed a flick so much, mon cheri.''
(Photograph No. 5).

There was then an interval of just over an hour before any
further members of the group came in.   The three couples referred
to above had supper in the Restaurant while the later comers only
arrived in time for drinks before the meeting.

At 12.28 Scab Wilson arrived and was followed immediately by Mug Masters. They were both spruced up for their visit to the Club but as soon as they opened their mouths anyone could tell that they'd spent most of their lives in Limehouse. The two having greeted each other, Masters said:

''What would you do, Scab, with a jane what you'd taken to the races for the day, given dinner at the Troc', stood five-bob seats at the pictures an' supper at the Corner House - wouldn't let you inside the door of her flat when you sees her home?''

Wilson replied: ''I'd thank me stars I 'ad the time off to play such games an' hope for better luck with my next piece of skirt. How'd you like yours truly's job - muckin' about in them quarries day after day - then having to jog up from Weymouth by a stop-at-all-stations because I missed the proper train?'' (Photograph No. 6).

At 12.35 Denis Burke, alias O'Leary, arrived. He gave me a surly, suspicious look as he signed the book and hurried inside without speaking. (Photograph No. 7).

At 12.42 Mr. and Mrs. Patrick Murphy and Sean Connolly arrived together; all three very friendly. Murphy looked at the clock above my desk and remarked: ''Just in time for a round of drinks before we get down to business.''

Connolly replied: ''Now, take it easy, Pat. Isn't it the best part of a bottle you've put away already? If you don't do

as I told you at exactly the right moment, the whole lot of us
may be for it.''

''Sure, an' I'll take it easy,'' said Murphy.   ''What time
is zero hour?''

''Just as soon as we're all set,'' answered Connolly.   I
repeated my comic line; Connolly gave me his genial smile and
Murphy looked faintly amused, but I don't think the lady got it.
(Photograph No. 8).

The whole of the above conversation took place in Erse,
which I speak a little and understand quite well as I lived in
Western Ireland for over five years when I was a young man.

At 12.48 William (Big Bill) Benson arrived.   He appeared
thoughtful and pre-occupied.   As he signed he threw a 10/- note
on my desk without even glancing up.   The entrance fee is 7/6 so
I produced 2/6 change but he impatiently waved it aside and strode
into the Club.   (Photograph No. 9).

His arrival completed the assembly of the group; all
sixteen of its members then being somewhere inside the Club.

At 12.54 the band had just stopped playing and I distinctly
heard two shots and a scream in the interior of the Club.   I
immediately ran to the door of the Restaurant.   Most of the
guests were on their feet and all present, including members of
the staff, were staring in the direction of the storeroom.

A military-looking man, in white tie and tails, and a young
girl, who looked like a debutante, were standing up at a

table near me.

Suddenly he seized her by the arm and cried: ''Come on! I must get you out of this!''

Upon which the two of them ran towards me, and this started the stampede.

I attempted to close the restaurant doors, but everyone inside seemed to have taken fright at the same moment. They came at me in a solid mass and I was bowled over, striking my head on the corner of my desk as I fell, which caused me to become unconscious.

In my brief glimpse of the restaurant and the oncoming crowd I did not actually see any members of the I.R.A. group, but one or more of them must have left by the Curzon Street entrance among the mob, after I was knocked down.

I regained consciousness at 1.3 a.m., to find Detective-Officer Goddard sponging my face. He later accompanied me, on Detective Inspector MacKechnie's instructions, back to the Yard to make this report before going into the sanatorium.

Having been informed that the shop-front of No. 94 Shepherd's Market was blown in with explosives at 12.58, while I was unconscious, may I suggest that, since this occurred within four minutes of the shooting of Orloff, it appears to have been planned beforehand.

In this connection I would draw attention to the conversation between Murphy and Connolly reported herein. ''The right

moment'' referred to by Connolly may have been the shooting of
Orloff, and the job Murphy had to be ready to do, have been the
blowing in of the shop-front in Shepherd's Market.

In my view the explosion was planned with a double motive.
(1) In order that it would cause a panic in the restaurant, if the
shots failed to do so, and enable the murderer to get away
unnoticed in the ensuing confusion. (2) To enable those members
of the group who were already locked in the secret room to get
clear of the premises before the police could come on the scene.

I have the honour to be, Sir,

Your obedient servant,

E. D. Spigott

Detective-Sergeant, Special Branch.

From Detective Inspector

J. D. MacKechnie (continued)

I cannot agree with Detective-Sergeant Spigott's deduction
from the Murphy-Connolly conversation. Why should the I.R.A.
group Chief plan to eliminate Orloff on a night when there was
a full meeting of the group, and thus expose them all to possible
capture?

It seems to me more probable that Orloff's connection with
us was only discovered when the majority of the group had already
gathered in the secret room.

Possibly the murderer had even learned that a raid was

imminent, and shot Orloff not only out of revenge, but to create an alarm which would ensure his associates getting clear of the Club before the police arrived.

In any case, I feel that the murder of Orloff was decided upon as an emergency measure, and there was neither time nor opportunity to warn the people already in the secret room. And that these, alarmed by the shots which they took as a signal that the Club was being raided, and finding themselves trapped, decided to force their way out via the shop by blowing in its boarded-up window; in spite of the big risk that by doing so they might have detonated their whole store of explosives.

Fortunately, Spigott's camera was not damaged during the melee in the entrance of the Club at 12.55-59, and, as reported, he had succeeded in taking a complete series of photographs of all the members of the group as they entered the Club earlier in the evening.

These have been developed, and prints are forwarded herewith; also all particulars we have to date of the originals.

Orloff being dead, the group is now reduced to fifteen in number. In view of the warning message found in his trouser pocket, it is clear that he was killed by one of his associates, because one or more of them knew that he was squealing to us. Moreover, the warning message indicates that his murderer was the leader of the group.

Unfortunately, as Spigott was knocked out in the first rush

of guests from the Club he is unable to inform us which members of the group left among the panicking crowd, and we have no means, apart from the clues secured, of ascertaining which members of the group were already in the secret room at the time of the murder.

In consequence we have, at present, no evidence upon which we can formulate a charge against any member of the group, with the one exception of O'Leary, alias Burke, who is wanted in connection with the Hammersmith Bridge outrage.

Our problems, therefore, are:

(A) To identify Orloff's murderer, which, as we have good grounds for believing him to be the brains behind the group, would in all probability break it up.

(B) To establish the identity of those members of the group who were in the secret room at 12.54 a.m., as each individual who can be proved to have been in that room can be charged with conspiracy and complicity in the manufacture of infernal machines for felonious purposes; which would result in our being able to put them away for from three to ten years.

Having traced all fifteen members of the group on information supplied by Spigott since his installation at the Club, we were able to bring them all in for questioning before 3 a.m.

All admit to having visited the Milky Way last night between the hours of 10 p.m. and 12.50 a.m. But all declare that they left the Club by its proper entrance in Curzon Street among the panicking crowd that rushed out on hearing the shots that killed .

Orloff, and the subsequent explosion.

Further, all fifteen deny ever having been in the secret room, forming part of 94, Shepherd's Market, and all knowledge of its existence.

Unless, therefore, the signatures of the suspects (taken at the Yard), photographs taken by Spigott (and others) and latest information secured to date regarding the members of the group, all of which are enclosed herewith, can be construed as positive evidence against any or all of the prisoners, we shall be compelled to release them.

I am, however, holding them, pending your instructions.

I have the honour to be, Sir,

Your obedient servant,

J. D. MacKechnie

Detective Inspector, Special Branch.

Carlotta Casado.

Kathleen Murphy

Denis Burke

Argyle Sullivan

Patrick Murphy.

Heinrich Hauser

A.B.Masters

Huson de Lys.

William Benson

Henry Wilson

Karl Finnigan

Toby Bandenay

Sean Connolly

Terrance Boyd-O'Dare

Pauline Victor

Exhibit A

Exhibit B

Exhibit C

Exhibit D

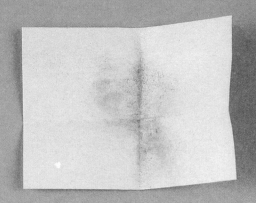

Exhibit E

Dear Masters,

This is to inform you that the next full Meeting, at which your presence is required is to take place at the Curzon Street Headquarters on the night of the 23rd-24th instant. We shall sit down to business at 1 o'clock, so you should be in the Club by 12.45.

Exhibit F

CARLTON
CINEMA
S.W.1
23/5/
8.
Royal
B
To be retained

CARLTON
CINEMA
S.W.1
23/5/39
8.30
Royal Circle
8/6
B 19
To be retained

Exhibit G

23. 5. 1939

Exhibit H

Exhibit I

Exhibit J

Exhibit K

Exhibit L

Exhibit M

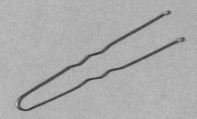

Exhibit N

Exhibit O

WATCH OUT! THIS AFTERNOON I OVERHEARD TWO OF THEM SAY THEY THINK THERE'S SOMETHING PHONY ABOUT THE NEW DOOR PORTER. REMEMBER WHAT THE BIG BOY SAID HE'D DO IF WE PLAYED HIM ANY TRICKS. IF THEY CONVINCE HIM THAT THEY'RE RIGHT HE'LL RUB YOU OUT.

Exhibit P

Photograph No. 1. TONY PENDENNYS

The particulars regarding Tony Pendennys which are given in the
script have, of course, no reference whatever to Lord Poulett, who very
kindly posed for this photograph

Photograph No. 2. CARLOTTA CASADO

The particulars regarding Carlotta Casado which are given in the script
have, of course, no reference whatever to Miss Doris Zinkeisen (Mrs.
Grahame Johnstone) who very kindly posed for this photograph

Photograph No. 3. ANGELA SULLIVAN AND HEINRICH HÄUSER

The particulars regarding Angela Sullivan and Heinrich Häuser which
are given in the script have, of course, no reference whatever to Christabel,
Lady Ampthill, and Sir Malcolm Campbell, who very kindly posed for
this photograph

Photograph No. 4. KARL FINIGAN AND PAULINE VIDOR

The particulars regarding Karl Finigan and Pauline Vidor which are given in the script have, of course, no reference whatever to Mr. Charles Birkin and Miss Eve Chaucer (Mrs. Dennis Wheatley), who very kindly posed for this photograph

Photograph No. 5. NINON DE LYS AND TERRANCE BOYD-O'DARE

The particulars regarding Ninon de Lys and Terrance Boyd-O'Dare
which are given in the script have, of course, no reference whatever to
Miss Diana Younger and Captain E. H. Tattersall, who very kindly posed
for this photograph

Photograph No. 6. "SCAB" WILSON AND "MUG" MASTERS

The particulars regarding "Scab" Wilson and "Mug" Masters which
are given in the script have, of course, no reference whatever to Mr.
Dennis Wheatley and Mr. J. G. Links, who posed for this photograph

Photograph No. 7. DENIS BURKE alias RORY O'LEARY

The particulars regarding Denis Burke, alias Rory O'Leary, which are
given in the script have, of course, no reference whatever to Lord Donegall
who very kindly posed for this photograph

**Photograph No. 8. PATRICK MURPHY, KATHLEEN MURPHY
AND SEAN CONNOLLY**

The particulars regarding Patrick Murphy, Kathleen Murphy and Sean
Connolly which are given in the script have, of course, no reference what-
ever to Mr. Gilbert Frankau, Lady Stanley of Alderley and Sir Harry
Brittain, who very kindly posed for this photograph

Photograph No. 9. A PAGE AND WILLIAM BENSON

The particulars regarding William Benson which are given in the script
have, of course, no reference whatever to Mr. Peter Cheyney, who very
kindly posed for this photograph

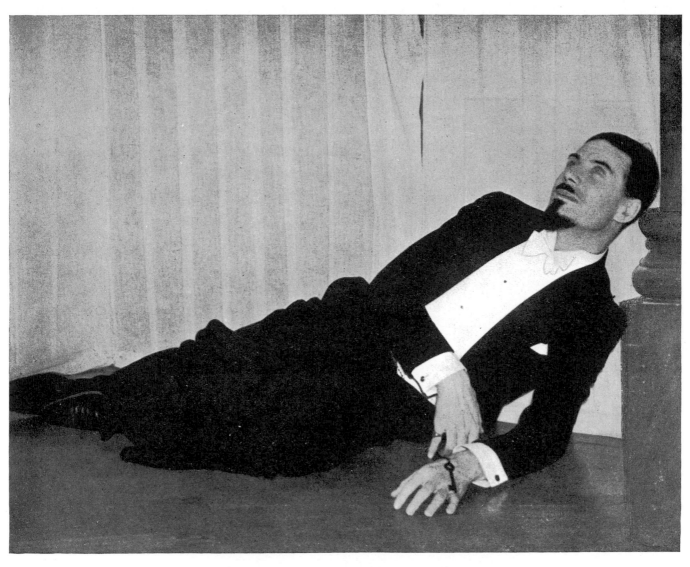

Photograph No. 10. SERGE ORLOFF

The particulars regarding Serge Orloff which are given in the script
have, of course, no reference whatever to Mr. Val Gielgud, who very
kindly posed for this photograph

TABLE IN SECRET ROOM BEHIND MILKY WAY CLUB
As left at 12.56 a.m., 24/5/39

Note. The piece of white paper near the large circular ash-tray on the table is Exhibit C, a doodle, but the markings on it (as is always the case with blue ink) failed to come out in the photograph. The small irregular white patch between the top hat and the triangular ash-tray is Exhibit D.

Photograph No. 1.　TONY PENDENNYS

Particulars ascertained up to 24 /5 /39

Age:　　30.
Height:　5' 7".
Build:　Strong.　Broad shouldered.
Eyes:　Hazel.
Hair:　　Light brown; slightly wavy.

Born at Horsham, Sussex, the only son of Andrew Pendennys, J.P.,
LL.D.　Educated Milton and Sandhurst, but left Military College on
father's death in 1928.　Inherited money, but lost it in 1930
slum p through bad speculations.　Meanwhile had been studying music.
First appeared in band at Ciro's in 1930.　Worked under Raymond
Hicks on tour 1931-1932.　From 1933 to 1935 ran own dance band for
private engagements.　1936 toured Continent.　Arrested in Marseilles June 1936 with Emile Corot and Lucille Verlaine at the
Restaurant de Réserve.　All three were charged with dope
smuggling.　Corot received a three-year sentence, the woman
Verlaine eighteen months, but Pendennys was acquitted.　Shortly
afterwards he sailed for the United States where he remained till
April 1938.　On his return to England he went into partnership
with Orloff and has since been responsible for the band at the
Milky Way.

Address:　54, Gilbert Street, Grosvenor Square, W.1.

Photograph No. 2.   CARLOTTA CASADO

Particulars ascertained up to 24 /5 /39

Age: (about) 31.
Height: 5' 7".
Build: Slight.
Eyes: Dark blue.
Hair: Black.
Complexion: Sun-tanned.

Comes from a good Spanish family who are natives of Catalonia.
Her father was Professor of Physics at Barcelona University.   He
held strong Liberal and Separatist views, on account of which he
was imprisoned by Primo de Rivera in 1928, but was released and
reinstated in his professorship on the Dictator's fall, 1930.
Carlotta early became interested in political movements and a
prominent personality among a group of young intellectuals.   In
1931 she joined the C.N.T. and in 1935 was elected a member of
the F.A.I., the inner ring which controlled the policy of the
Barcelona anarchists.   Her brother, Joseph, was a bad lot and,
after being disowned by the father, left Spain in 1934.   He has
since lived in Paris and London, mixing with a rather dubious
crowd and picking up a precarious living in various night-haunts
as a professional dancing partner.   Carlotta was largely
instrumental in organizing the Spanish People's Ballet, which held
its first Season in 1932, and it was through this that she met
Orloff during its fourth Season at San Sebastian in 1935, when he
was temporarily running the San Antonio Restaurant there.   The two
appear to have had a love affair.   Carlotta has never married and
there is reason to suppose that she is still in love with Orloff.
Spigott reports that Orloff is keeping Nerina Jolliff, one of his
dance hostesses, and that this was not known to Carlotta until
the night of the raid, when high words passed between the two
women.   In the Spanish Civil War Carlotta worked in a Barcelona
Hospital and organized entertainments for the troops.   Three days
before the city fell to General Franco she left it as a refugee
and came, via Marseilles and Calais, to join her brother in
England.   Orloff then engaged her to run his cabarets at the
Milky Way and she has worked there ever since.   The brother, a
very good-looking man of 28, who is known among his friends as
''Spanish Joe'', was deported on the 10th April last on suspicion
of being concerned with the traffic in illicit drugs.

Address: 10b, Willingham Mansions, Maida Vale, W.9.

Photograph No. 3.   ANGELA SULLIVAN (left)

Particulars ascertained up to 24/5/39

Age: 38.
Height: 5' 8".
Build: Strong, with good figure.
Eyes: Blue.
Hair: Golden brown.
Complexion: Fair.

Born in Littlefold, Hampshire, England.   Only daughter of
late Canon H. T. Brentwick, D.D.   Served as V.A.D. in last
year of Great War.   While nursing met Bryan Sullivan, a
wounded officer, whom she married when still only 17.   After
the Armistice the couple went to live at Ballyvaghan, Co. Clare,
Ireland, Sullivan's home.   He was fanatically anti-English on
the Irish question and narrowly escaped being shot in October
1919 by the Black and Tans.   He fled to the hills where he
operated with a band of Irregulars for some time.   For further
particulars of his anti-British activities, which have continued
ever since, see his Dossier;   the last entry of which is ''found
guilty of participation in the Liverpool bomb outrages and
sentenced to seven years penal servitude.   10.2.39.''   The
Sullivans are a most devoted couple and as she married so young
she quickly became imbued with his fanatical ideas.   Except for
occasional trips to this country and abroad she has lived in
Ireland for the last 20 years.   She was in Liverpool for her
husband's trial and has remained here since.

Address: The Rembrant Hotel, Buckingham Palace Road, S.W.1.

<u>Photograph No. 3.   HEINRICH HAUSER (right)</u>

Particulars ascertained up to 24 /5 /39

Age: 50.
Height: 5' 10".
Build: Wiry.
Eyes: Very clear bright blue.
Hair: Dark brown, straight.

Häuser is a native of the Rhineland, born near Coblentz.   He was
gazetted to the 16th Ulhaus in 1909 and served with his regiment
up to the latter stages of the War.   He was mentioned twice in
despatches, received the Iron Cross 2nd Class and, in 1916, promoted to the rank of Captain.   Most of his war service was on the
Russian front and the Division to which he was attached was
among those immobilised in the Ukraine on the outbreak of the
Revolution.   These troops were so corrupted by Bolshevik propa-
ganda that they could not be withdrawn for service on other fronts
for fear they would contaminate loyal Divisions.   When food
difficulties arose many of the Units disintegrated, became
independent robber bands or took sides with either the Reds or
Whites in the Russian Civil War.   As the Whites were supported
by the Allies, Häuser joined the Bolsheviks and led a detachment
of Reds against General Yudenitch in Esthonia.   He then disappeared for some time, doubtless preferring not to return to his
own country after the War was over, as he reappeared again in 1920
as a member of Trotsky's staff.   It was about this time that
he met Orloff and the two worked together until 1924 when Häuser
returned to Germany.   He settled in Berlin and earned a precarious living by writing articles for a number of Socialist
papers, at once identifying himself with the same political
movement.   In 1933, when the tide had turned definitely in favour
of the Nazis, Häuser emigrated to the States where he continued
to earn his living by journalism.   In 1937 he joined the
Dragenberg Press Agency's organisation there, and in January 1939
was transferred by them to their London office.

Address: 104, Tite Street, Chelsea, S.W.3.

Photograph No. 4.   KARL FINIGAN (left)

Particulars ascertained up to 24/5/39

Age: 38.
Height: 5' 10".
Build: Slight.
Eyes: Hazel.
Hair: Dark; snow-white at temples and peak.

Finigan's father was a landowner with an estate outside Dublin,
where he bred large numbers of horses.   His principal customer,
in the late '90's and up to the outbreak of the Great War, was
the German Army.   For the purpose of negotiating sales he paid
frequent visits to Germany, where he met and married Fräulein
Greta Häuser, Heinrich Häuser's aunt.   He joined the Rebels and
was killed defending the Dublin Post Office in the Easter
Rebellion of 1915.   Finigan, then a boy of 14, was adopted by
his uncle, Clancy Finigan, who had settled in America some years
earlier, and went to live in the States with him.   Karl was
educated by his uncle at Gretton and Yale.   He has published four
books of poetry and for the last seventeen years has divided his
interests between the artistic set in which he moves in New York
and the American societies for the maintenance of Irish Independence.   Owing to the manner of his father's death he is
extremely bitter against the British.   He has paid seven visits
to Ireland in the last six years and it was during one of these
that he spent a night in a haunted house, which resulted in his
hair turning prematurely white overnight.   He presumably contacted his cousin, Häuser, when the German went as a journalist
to the United States.

Address: 6, Queen Charlotte's Mansions, Westminster, S.W.1.

Note.   Spigott has telephoned from the sanatorium to add to his
         report that up to the 23rd inst. Finigan wore his hair long
         and full in the fashion of an Edwardian poet but that he had
         evidently had it cut to moderate length that day;   as seen
         in the photograph taken that night.

<u>Photograph No. 4.   PAULINE VIDOR (right)</u>

Particulars ascertained up to 24/5/39

Age: 40.
Height: 5' 5".
Build: Medium strong; good figure.
Eyes: Green, with yellow specks.
Hair: Cendrée blonde, going white.
Complexion: Very fair.

Born in Poland, married 1924 Count Ladislas Vidor, from whom she obtained a divorce in 1930.   Went to live in Paris in 1931, where she became a prominent figure in literary and artistic circles. Removed to the United States in 1935 and settled in New York. Has many friends among American artists, poets and painters and thus, presumably, met Finigan.   How long they have been acquainted is unknown.   They arrived together from America in the S.S. Washington on November 24th, 1938, spent three weeks in Dublin and on reaching London took the furnished flat where they are now living together.   Madame Vidor is a crack shot and frequently goes down to Bisley to practise revolver shooting.

Address: 6, Queen Charlotte's Mansions, Westminster, S.W.1.

Photograph No. 5.   NINON DE LYS (left)

Particulars ascertained up to 24/5/39

Age: 20 (Appears older owing to use of heavy
Height: 5' 4".   make-up).
Build: Very slim and supple.
Eyes: Grey.   Lashes very heavily blacked.
Hair: Golden, natural blonde.
Complexion: Fair and flawless.

Born at Sables d'Or, Brittany.   Studied dancing at Children's
Academy, Dinard, from age of 6.   Toured France with troupe
''Petites Belles de Bretagne,'' 1931-1932.   Joined Ecole Terpsi-
core in Paris, 1933.   Made first solo appearance at Biarritz in
summer of 1936; was immediate success.   Many good engagements
on Continent since.   First visit to England May - July 1938.
Returned for further engagements, January 1939.   Recreations,
riding and flying.   Has acquired among many others the following
friends here: Air Vice-Marshal Fulchard, Lord Hudderstone,
Mr. R. C. Bingden-Brown (Home Office), Wing-Commander Rowland
Roylance and Mr. G. B. Lake, of Molden Manor, Leicestershire.
She is not suspected of espionage activities but it is believed
that Boyd-O'Dare may be obtaining information through her from
Bingden-Brown and others.

Address: 42, Albert Gate Court, Knightsbridge, S.W.1.

Photograph No. 5.   CAPTAIN TERRANCE BOYD-O'DARE (right)

Particulars ascertained up to 24/5/39

Age: 42.
Height: 6' 1".
Build: Strong.
Eyes: Blue.
Hair: Straight; fair.

Boyd-O'Dare comes from an old Ulster family, having long associa-
tions with the Army; but his mother was a Donelly from County
Kildare.   The mother being a Roman Catholic the boy was brought
up in that faith and he spent most of his youth with his mother's
people in Southern Ireland.   His father insisted, however, that
he should go into the family Regiment, The Royal Ulster Rifles,
and he was gazetted to it straight from the O.T.C. of his Public
School in January 1915.   He served in France and was wounded on
the Somme in July 1916.   Evacuated to England he spent a period
in Hospitals and Convalescent Depots, after which he was sent out
again, this time to the Salonica front, and was promoted to the
rank of Captain.   He proved a keen soldier and was popular with
his men; but his caustic wit, which he often exercised at the
expense of all things connected with Northern Ireland, proved a
constant irritation to his brother officers.   This developed
into a definite antagonism during the after-war years as the
tension between Northern and Southern Ireland increased.   The
sympathies of the Regiment were naturally with the north while
Boyd-O'Dare, becoming more and more under the influence of his
mother's relatives, espoused more strongly than ever the cause
of the South.   In June 1926 there was an open quarrel in which
Boyd-O'Dare struck a brother officer.   At the Court of Enquiry
which followed he urged extreme provocation but was severely
reprimanded, upon which he sent in his papers.   This abrupt
termination of his military career has since been regarded by him
as grounds for a bitter grudge against Britain.   By 1928 we
found that he had become involved with the I.R.A., and his dossier
will provide particulars of his activities in the movement since.
He last arrived in England on December 22nd, 1938.

Address: No. 10 Flat, 34, St. James Place, S.W.1.

Photograph No. 6.   HENRY WILSON (left)

Particulars ascertained up to 24/5/39

Age: 42.
Height: 5' 8".
Build: Thick.
Eyes: Brown.
Hair: Dark brown, straight.

Wilson, known among his associates as ''Scab'', is an habitual
criminal.   He was first arrested on a pickpocketing charge in
1909, and subsequent offences led to his being sent to Borstal.
From the Institution he went straight into the Army as a volunteer
shortly after the outbreak of the Great War.   Although then still
under 18, he showed considerable ability and achieved the rank of
Company Quarter-master Sergeant three years later.   In 1918
when his Battalion was in the Ypres sector it was discovered
that he was selling surplus Army rations to the Belgian civilians
behind the line, upon which he was court-martialed and reduced
to the ranks.   In March 1919 he was demobilised and acquired a
tobacco and newspaper shop in Stepney.   In January 1921 the
business failed and with it, apparently, ended any attempt on
''Scab's'' part to go straight.   The following April he was
arrested for complicity in a burglary and received an eighteen-
months' sentence.   From this time on, as his dossier will show,
he has been constantly in and out of prison.   Hitherto all the
charges made against him have been in connection with burglary
and for some years past he has specialised in safe-blowing.   As
one of the few crooks who have a thorough knowledge of explosives
and the courage to employ them, he gets a big cut after each
successful robbery.   When out of prison he spends lavishly.
Last released (from Dartmoor) November 4th, 1938.

Address: 25, Rylands Road, Nottingdale, W.8.

Photograph No. 6.   A. B. MASTERS (right)

Particulars ascertained up to 24/5/39

Age: 34.
Height: 5' 9".
Build: Athletic.
Eyes: Dark brown.
Hair: Thick, black, wavy.

Masters is known among his associates as ''Mug'', which is a
shortening of his original nickname ''Handsome Mug''.   He first
came to our notice in 1927 as a racecourse crook and soon after
became a member of the Rosini gang which levied blackmail on
bookmakers.   At Lingfield in 1930 the Rosini boys received a
particularly bad beating-up from their rivals, the Levinsky gang.
Two deaths resulted and a number of serious wounds from razor-
slashings and, after this, Masters apparently decided that the
race-game was not worth the candle.   As a member of the Cock-
a-Hoop Athletic Club of Whitechapel, he had already won several
prizes for gymnastics and he now proceeded to adapt his physical
abilities to his criminal career.   A series of cat-burglaries
in the Richmond and Cheam area, in 1931-1933, entirely defeated
us until a Colonel Bingewell, returning to his house late one
night after an Old Comrades dinner, found Masters in his bedroom
and laid him out with a whisky decanter.   Masters has been inside
on two similar charges since and was last released (from Dartmoor)
on February 9th of this year.   He has a peculiar fascination
for women and treats those in whom he becomes interested well,
but he has never married.

Address: 57, Goldhawk Road, Wanstead, E.17.

Photograph No. 7.   RORY O'LEARY alias DENIS BURKE

Particulars ascertained up to 24/5/39

Age: 36.
Height: 5' 8".
Build: Slight.
Eyes: Dark brown.
Hair: Dark brown; straight.

O'Leary is a native of Cork.   His father was a merchant of good
standing in that city and he lived with his wife and family in
a commodious mansion outside it.   During the troubles after the
War the O'Learys sheltered several Nationalist gunmen who were
on the run there.   The Black and Tans raided the place and, in
the ensuing gunfight, O'Leary, his wife and his eldest son were
all killed.   Young Rory disappeared and it was later learned that
he had run away to sea.   For seven years he served in numerous
ships, during the latter period as assistant ship's carpenter, but
there is no doubt that witnessing the massacre of his family left
an indelible impression on his mind.   He returned to Ireland
in 1929 and at once associated himself with the more reckless
elements of the old anti-British factions.   A record of his
activities, as known to us, will be found in his dossier.   His
hobby, learnt at sea, is wood carving and he has fashioned some
remarkably good reproductions of fine eighteenth-century furniture
for his home, which is outside Cork, about two miles from his
parents' old residence.   He is believed to have married a girl
named Maureen O'Shea in 1934, but we have no actual proof of
this.   In any case, they parted in less than a year, which
caused him to become misanthropic.   He is shrewd, daring and
unscrupulous in what he considers to be the cause of his country.
It is believed that many of the Tube Station outrages were
planned by him and we have definite proof that he was concerned in
the Hammersmith Bridge affair.

Address: 108, Acacia Road, St. John's Wood, N.W.8.

Photograph No. 8.   PATRICK MURPHY (left)

Particulars ascertained up to 24/5/39

Age: 51.
Height: 5' 10".
Build: Slim, athletic.
Eyes: Brown.
Hair: Brown, going slightly grey; straight.

Murphy was born in Limerick.   His father, a doctor, sent him to
Trinity College, Dublin, but he failed to take his medical Degree
and entered the old established house of Philimore Flannery,
General Importers, in 1910.   He showed such promise that his
firm sent him on a tour of Australasia and the Far East in 1913.
His movements during the Great War are obscure, but he was in
New Guinea when the Australian Forces landed there and joined
them as an irregular in their attack on the German Colony.   We
next hear of him in German East, where he offered his services
to General Smuts but, for some reason unknown, they were rejected.
This appears to have soured him against the British as he then
joined Von.Letow and fought for the remainder of the War on the
side of Germany.   Shortly after the Armistice he married a
German girl in Tanganyika and returned to Europe with her in
1922.   They settled in Bremen, where he entered the business of
her family; the Deutscher Kunst Allgemeine Gesellschaft; but in
1927 she was killed, as the result of a motor accident, upon which
he returned to Ireland.   During a series of visits to London he
utilised his German connections to negotiate an arrangement with
Acton Goddard & Sons, Fancy Goods Importers, of 24, Mincing Lane,
E.C.3, becoming a Director of the firm.   He has remained with them
ever since and, taking out British naturalization papers in 1930,
he settled in London.   He is responsible to his firm for the
marketing of their goods in the Irish Free State and has
doubtless used this to cover his I.R.A. activities.   In 1932 he
married Kathleen Deleney.

Address : 86, Hertford Street, Park Lane, W.1.

Photograph No. 8.   KATHLEEN MURPHY (centre)

Age: 29.
Height: 5' 3".
Build: Small, slim.
Eyes: Grey-blue.
Hair: Fair chestnut.
Complexion: Fair.

Mrs. Murphy is the only child of the late Major Markham Deleney, Lowlands Hall, Tipperary.   In the post-War troubles the Hall was used as a Headquarters by the Rebels and burnt down as a reprisal by the Black and Tans.   Major Deleney was absent abroad at the time and does not appear to have been a strong partisan of either one side or the other, but the event doubtless made a lasting impression on his small daughter who was only rescued from the fire with some difficulty.   From 1922 to 1924 the Deleneys lived in Dublin but in the latter year Kathleen was sent to school in Bournemouth and shortly afterwards her father bought a hotel there which he ran until he died in 1936.   Kathleen was married, from this hotel, in 1932 to Patrick Murphy and, as his wife, assumed British nationality.   It was doubtless on account of her father's hotel interest that Kathleen decided to run furnished apartments in London and the large house in Hertford Street was taken for that purpose.   Her father was able to send her numerous clients from Bournemouth and others were secured through their Irish connections.

Address: 86, Hertford Street, Park Lane, W.1.

Particulars ascertained up to 24/5/39

Age: 62.
Height: 6'.
Build: Strong.
Eyes: Brown.
Hair: Brown, turning grey; straight.

Connolly was born in Liverpool of Irish parents.   His father,
a lawyer, had strong Fenian sympathies, and Sean was brought up
in the belief that every interest in his life should be subord-
inated to the struggle for Irish independence.   By 1897 he was
already active in the Home Rule movement and openly declaring
his hatred of everything British.   He soon developed a remark-
able gift for oratory and between the late '90's and the outbreak
of the Great War addressed thousands of meetings on Home Rule
both in Liverpool and Ireland.   He was often in hiding from the
police, fought in the Easter Rebellion and, after its suppression,
led a band of Irregulars against the British.   In the following
years he was reported again and again as the organizer of surprise
raids in which the Black and Tans sustained many casualties;
but he was never caught.   He was an intimate friend of Michael
Collins but later they quarrelled and Connolly continued his
subversive activities.   Only failing health brought his long
career of fanatical patriotic violence to an apparent conclusion
when he left Ireland to settle in South Africa, in November 1937.
The date of his return to Europe is still unknown but his health
seems to have been much improved by his stay abroad.

Address: 86, Hertford Street, Park Lane, W.1.

Photograph No. 9.   WILLIAM HUGO BENSON

Particulars ascertained up to 24/5/39

Age: 42.
Height: 6' 2".
Build: Broad and powerful.
Eyes: Light blue.
Hair: Fair.

Benson was born in London but educated in Canada, where his father
had big timber interests.   On the outbreak of war he returned
to England, was granted a Commission in the Rutland Light Infantry
and proceeded to France in May 1915.   He was wounded and
invalided home the following October and not fit for active
service again until August 1918, when he went out once more as
a Captain.   After the Armistice he joined the White Russians.
For nearly two years he fought with them against the Bolsheviks
until he was captured during the sack of Rostov, tortured by the
Reds and narrowly escaped with his life.   Returning to Canada
in 1921, he quarrelled with his father through refusing to settle
down and go into the timber business.   Instead he engaged in
bootlegging across the Great Lakes and, later, took to rum-
running from the Bahamas.   In 1925 the Federals sank a steamer
he had chartered, with its whole cargo, and this put him out of
the business.   A year later he was arrested for gun-running in
Morocco but he escaped from prison before his trial.   Between
1926 and 1931 he participated in several Central and South
American Revolutions and civil wars.   In 1932 he appeared in
China and it was there that he became known as ''Big Bill''.
He fought for several prominent Chinese War Lords in the ensuing
years and ran a munitions factory at Hankow from May 1936, out
of which he made considerable profits, until it was destroyed
by the Japanese.   In October 1938 he returned to England with
a bank balance of less than £200 to show for all his years of
adventuring. He is, however, now in clover again, as last week
his father died and, apparently, relenting, left him the bulk
of his estate which is estimated to produce over a quarter of
a million pounds.

Address: The Wellington Hotel, Lancaster Gate, W.2.

Photograph No. 10. SERGE ORLOFF

Particulars ascertained up to 24/5/39

Age: 39.
Height: 5' 11".
Build: Slim.
Eyes: Brown.
Hair: Dark chestnut, wavy.   Small pointed
            Elizabethan beard of same colour.

Orloff was born in Kharkov.   His father was a restaurant
proprietor; his mother came from the lesser nobility.   As a boy
Serge showed unusual brilliance and his parents were ambitious
for him.   He entered the University of his native city before
he was seventeen.   There, he soon became a leader among the more
Radical students and was arrested as part-organizer of an anti-
Government demonstration at the end of his first term.   The
Revolution broke shortly afterwards and he immediately joined the
Red Guard.   In 1918, in spite of his youth, he was elected to
represent his Unit at a Council of Workmen and Soldiers in Moscow.
Here he met Trotsky, who was then organizing the Red Army.   The
War Lord took young Orloff on to his staff and sent him on
numerous special missions during the many months of Civil War
that followed.   Orloff was at different times Trotsky's personal
representative with the 2nd, 4th and 10th Armies, and was present
at the taking of Odessa, Rostov, Simbirsk and Orenberg.   After
the war he held a post in the supplies department of the Russian
War Office, until Trotsky's fall from power.   Orloff succeeded
in escaping the purge that followed, by slipping over the Finnish
border.   He then made his way to England, arriving here in
October 1928.   Joseph Toscani, an old friend of his father's,
gave him a job at the Cordon Bleu, and in 1930, on the head-
waiter's leaving, he became head-waiter there.   During 1934 and
1935 he held several temporary posts on the French and Italian
Rivieras and in Spain.   He then returned permanently to London
and opened his own place, the Milky Way.

Address: Flat b, 76, Half Moon Street, Piccadilly, W.1.

AUTHORS' NOTE ON HOW TO FILL IN READERS' MARK SHEETS

The joint authors, Messrs. Dennis Wheatley and J. G. Links, suggest that readers should now fill in the yellow form with their reasons for eliminating as many suspects as possible.

Seven suspects can each be *wholly* eliminated by *one* reason apiece. Seven more can each be *wholly* eliminated by *two* reasons apiece, or *partially* eliminated by *one* reason apiece.

For each suspect *wholly* eliminated you score *two* points, and for each only *partially* eliminated you score *one* point.

If fourteen suspects are eliminated correctly, but some of them only partially, the murderer can be identified as the only remaining suspect, and five points should be added to the score.

If fourteen suspects are wholly eliminated in complete accordance with the Assistant Commissioner's findings, and the murderer definitely identified, a further seven points should be added to the score ; the maximum score being forty points.

Eight solution sheets are provided, so that each member of the family may fill one up if they wish before the sealed page is cut. No peeping, now ! And we hope it will give you a lot of fun.

READER'S MARK SHEET

(See Authors' note on last page before Solution)

I eliminate the following suspects for the reasons stated below :

(Use two lines only in cases where you have more than one reason for eliminating a suspect.)

(1) ....

(2) ....

(3) ....

(4) ....

(5) ....

(6) ....

(7) ....

(8) (a) ....

    (b) ....

(9) (a) ....

    (b) ....

(10) (a) ....

     (b) ....

(11) (a) ....

     (b) ....

(12) (a) ....

     (b) ....

(13) (a) ....

     (b) ....

(14) (a) ....

     (b) ....

I identify Orloff's murderer as...

NOW REFER TO SOLUTION

Score **two** points for each suspect correctly eliminated by either one full or two
    partial reasons.

Score **one** point for each suspect only partially eliminated by one correct reason.

Score ....

If the murderer is correctly identified add five points to score.

If score now totals maximum (33 points) add further seven points to form
    Grand Total (40 points).   *Grand Total* ....

(Signed)...

READER'S MARK SHEET

(See Authors' note on last page before Solution)

I eliminate the following suspects for the reasons stated below :

(Use two lines only in cases where you have more than one reason for eliminating a suspect.)

(1) ....

(2) ....

(3) ....

(4) ....

(5) ....

(6) ....

(7) ....

(8) (a) ....

    (b) ....

(9) (a) ....

    (b) ....

(10) (a) ....

    (b) ....

(11) (a) ....

    (b) ....

(12) (a) ....

    (b) ....

(13) (a) ....

    (b) ....

(14) (a) ....

    (b) ....

I identify Orloff's murderer as ....

NOW REFER TO SOLUTION

Score **two** points for each suspect correctly eliminated by either one full or two partial reasons.

Score **one** point for each suspect only partially eliminated by one correct reason.

Score ....

If the murderer is correctly identified add five points to score.

If score now totals maximum (33 points) add further seven points to form Grand Total (40 points). *Grand Total* ....

(*Signed*)..

To

The Chief Commissioner.

Sir,

From the exhibits, photographs, and reports received in connection with the murder of Serge Orloff at or about 12.54 a.m. on the 24th instant, in the Milky Way Club, Curzon Street, Mayfair, we have now deduced the following:

The note of warning found upon Orloff's body establishes the motive of the murder, and clearly indicates that he was killed by one of the members of the I.R.A. group which used his premises as a rendezvous.

No member of that group who was admitted into the secret room by Orloff could have killed him, for the following reasons:

(A) As he admitted each person he relocked the door after them, and the door was locked when his body was found on the Club side of it.

(B) Once in the room they could not get back into the Club by way of the door, as we know from Orloff's statement that there were no duplicate keys to it; and his own was attached to his body.

(C) Neither could they get back to the Club by way of the shop in Shepherd's Market and walking round to its Curzon Street entrance, because the door of the shop was nailed up, and, when